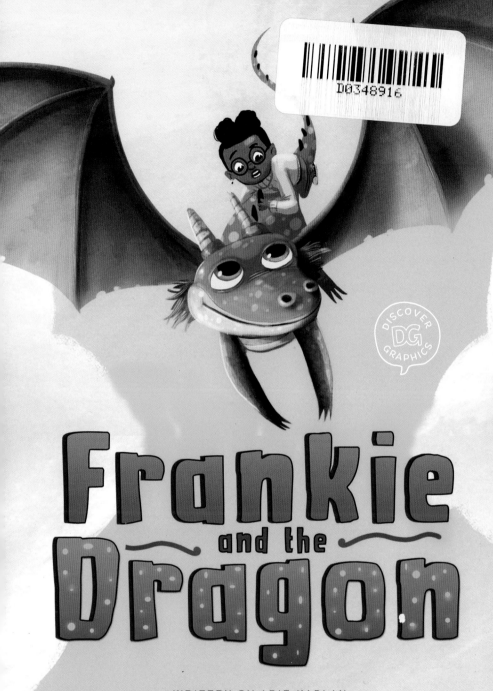

Frankie
and the
Dragon

WRITTEN BY ARIE KAPLAN

ILLUSTRATED BY CÉSAR SAMANEIGO

PICTURE WINDOW BOOKS
a capstone imprint

Discover Graphics is published by Picture Window Books,
an imprint of Capstone.
1710 Roe Crest Drive
North Mankato, Minnesota 56003
www.capstonepub.com

Library of Congress Cataloging-in-Publication Data
Names: Kaplan, Arie, author. | Samaneigo, Cesar, illustrator.
Title: Frankie the dragon / by Arie Kaplan ; illustrated by Cesar Samaneigo.
Description: North Mankato, Minnesota : Picture Window Books, a Capstone imprint, [2021] | Series: Discover graphics. Mythical creatures | Audience: Ages 5–7. | Audience: Grades K–1.
Identifiers: LCCN 2020031435 (print) | LCCN 2020031436 (ebook) | ISBN 9781515882015 (hardcover) | ISBN 9781515883067 (paperback) | ISBN 9781515891970 (pdf) | ISBN 9781515892564 (kindle edition)
Subjects: LCSH: Graphic novels. | CYAC: Graphic novels. | Dragons—Fiction. | Fear—Fiction. | Racially mixed people—Fiction.
Classification: LCC PZ7.7.K37 Fr 2021 (print) | LCC PZ7.7.K37 (ebook) | DDC 741.5/973—dc23
LC record available at https://lccn.loc.gov/2020031435
LC ebook record available at https://lccn.loc.gov/2020031

Summary: Frankie Marble is shy. She's too scared to enter the school talent show. But everything changes when she meets Bandit, the dog that is definitely not a dragon!

Editorial Credits:
Editor: Mari Bolte; Designer: Kay Fraser; Media Researcher: Tracy Cummins; Production Specialist: Katy LaVigne

To my daughter, Aviya Leah Kaplan, who is the real-life Frankie Marble. —AK

WORDS TO KNOW

cooped up—kept in a space that does not allow much freedom

portrait—a picture of a person usually showing the face

shy—being quiet or nervous in front of other people

Printed in the United States 3960

CAST OF CHARACTERS

Frankie "Pineapple" Marble is an ordinary girl. She likes to read and draw. She is shy.

Bandit is a dragon that Frankie finds at the park. She tries to trick people into thinking he is a dog.

Frankie's **Dad** and **Mom** love her very much. They know she's shy, but they support her in whatever she wants to do.

HOW TO READ A GRAPHIC NOVEL

Graphic novels are easy to read. Boxes called panels show you how to follow the story. Look at the panels from left to right and top to bottom.

Read the word boxes and word balloons from left to right as well. Don't forget the sound and action words in the pictures.

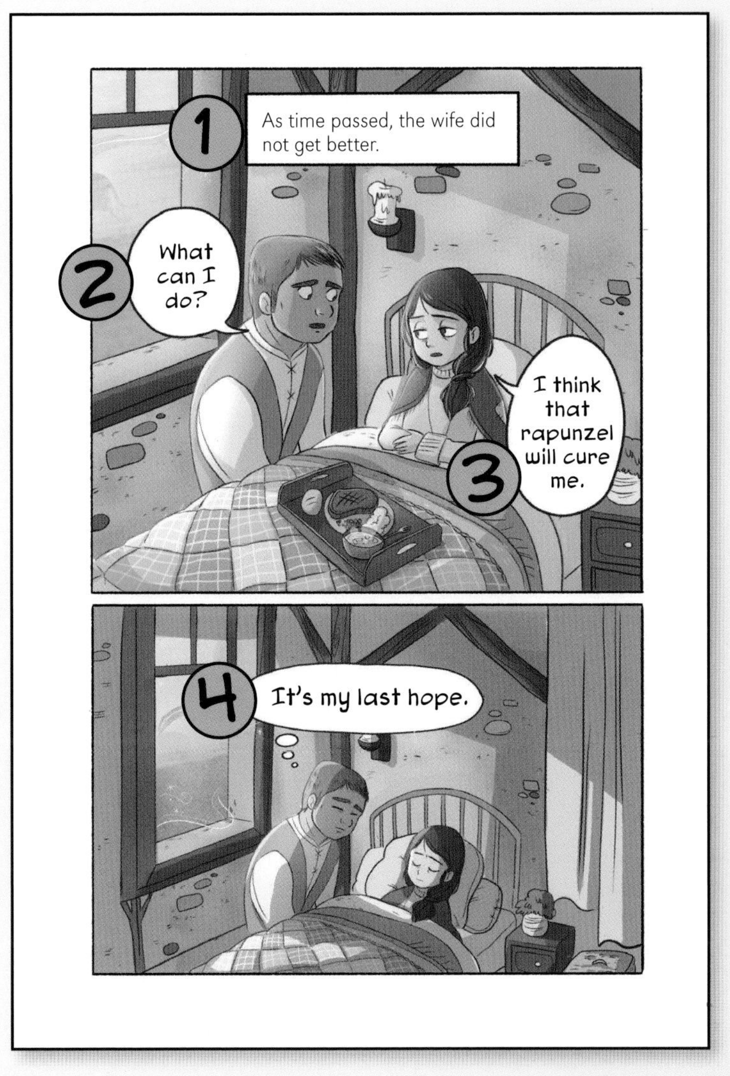
1
As time passed, the wife did not get better.
2
What can I do?
3
I think that rapunzel will cure me.
4
It's my last hope.

The pictures and the words work together to tell the whole story.

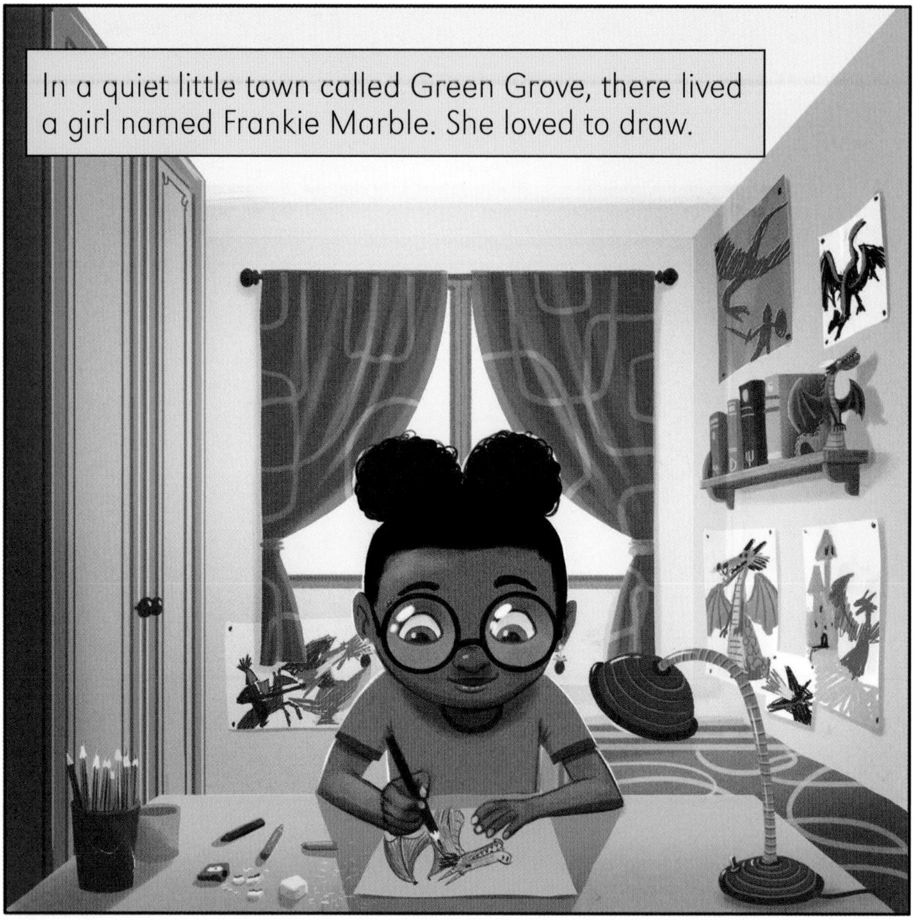
In a quiet little town called Green Grove, there lived a girl named Frankie Marble. She loved to draw.

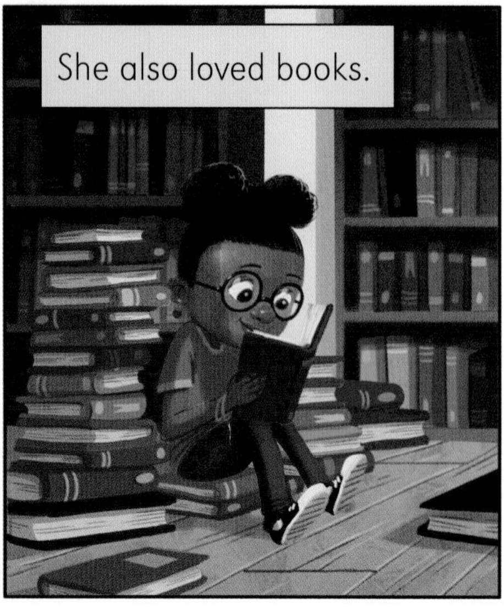
She also loved books.

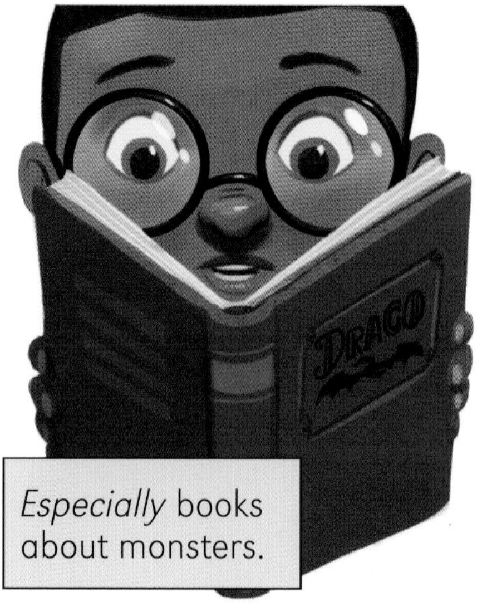
Especially books about monsters.

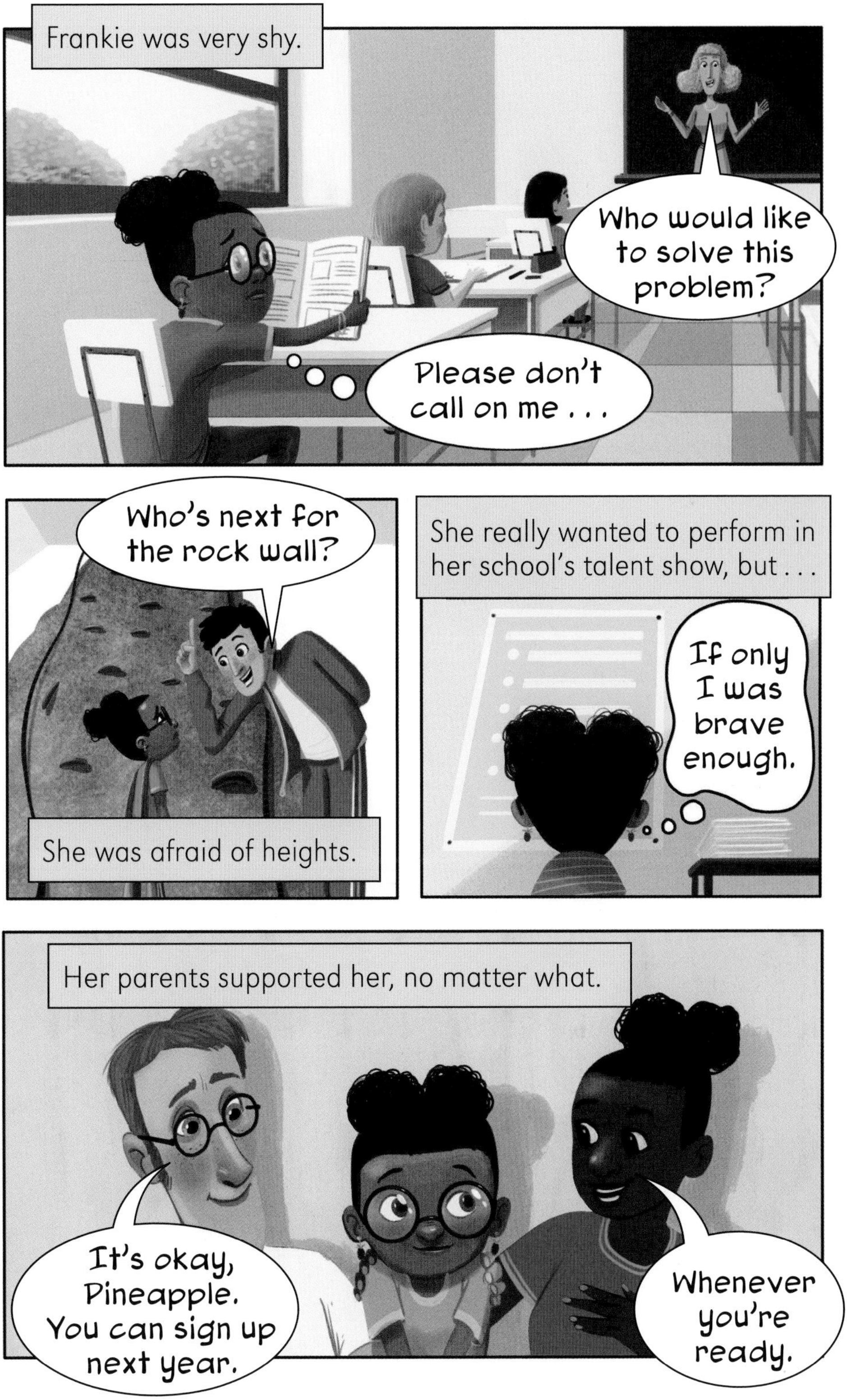
Frankie was very shy.
Who would like to solve this problem?
Please don't call on me . . .
Who's next for the rock wall?
She was afraid of heights.
She really wanted to perform in her school's talent show, but . . .
If only I was brave enough.
Her parents supported her, no matter what.
It's okay, Pineapple. You can sign up next year.
Whenever you're ready.

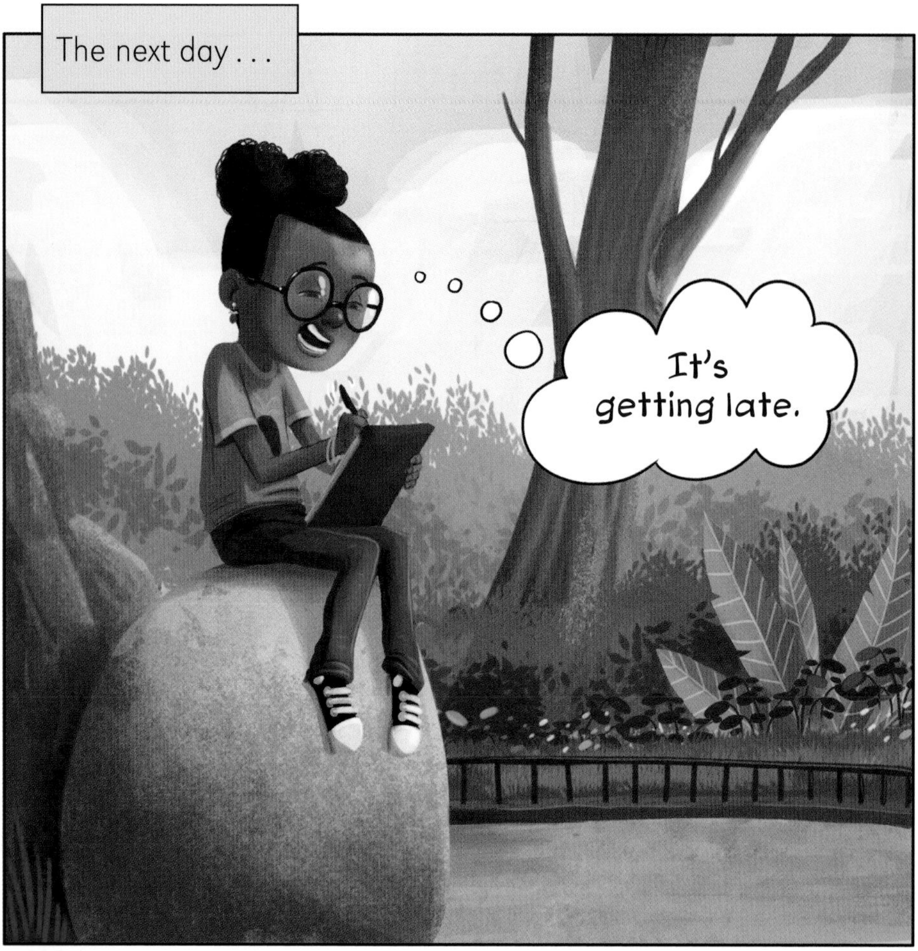
The next day . . .
It's getting late.

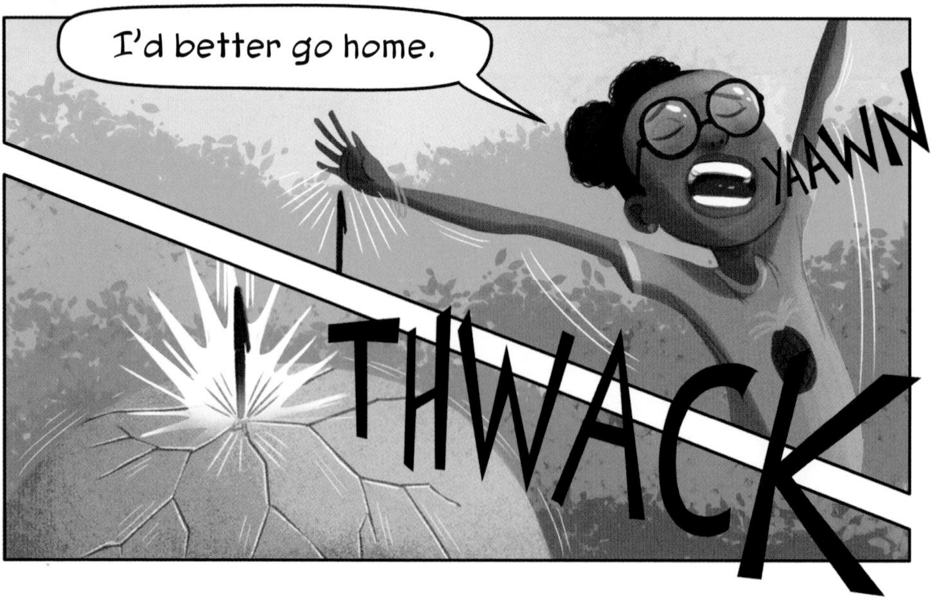
I'd better go home.
YAAWN
THWACK

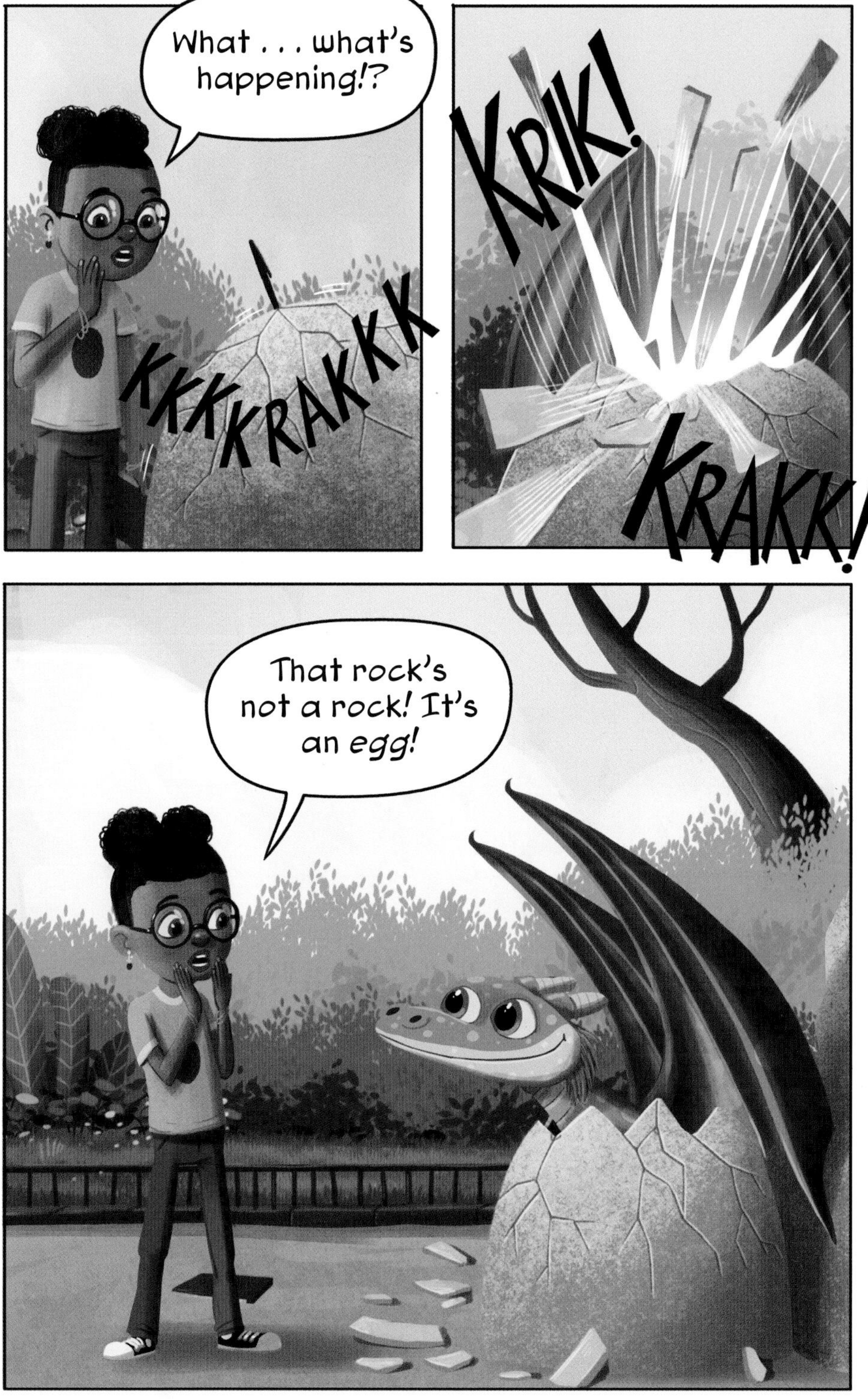
What . . . what's happening!?
KKKKRAKKK
KRIK!
KRAKK!
That rock's not a rock! It's an *egg*!

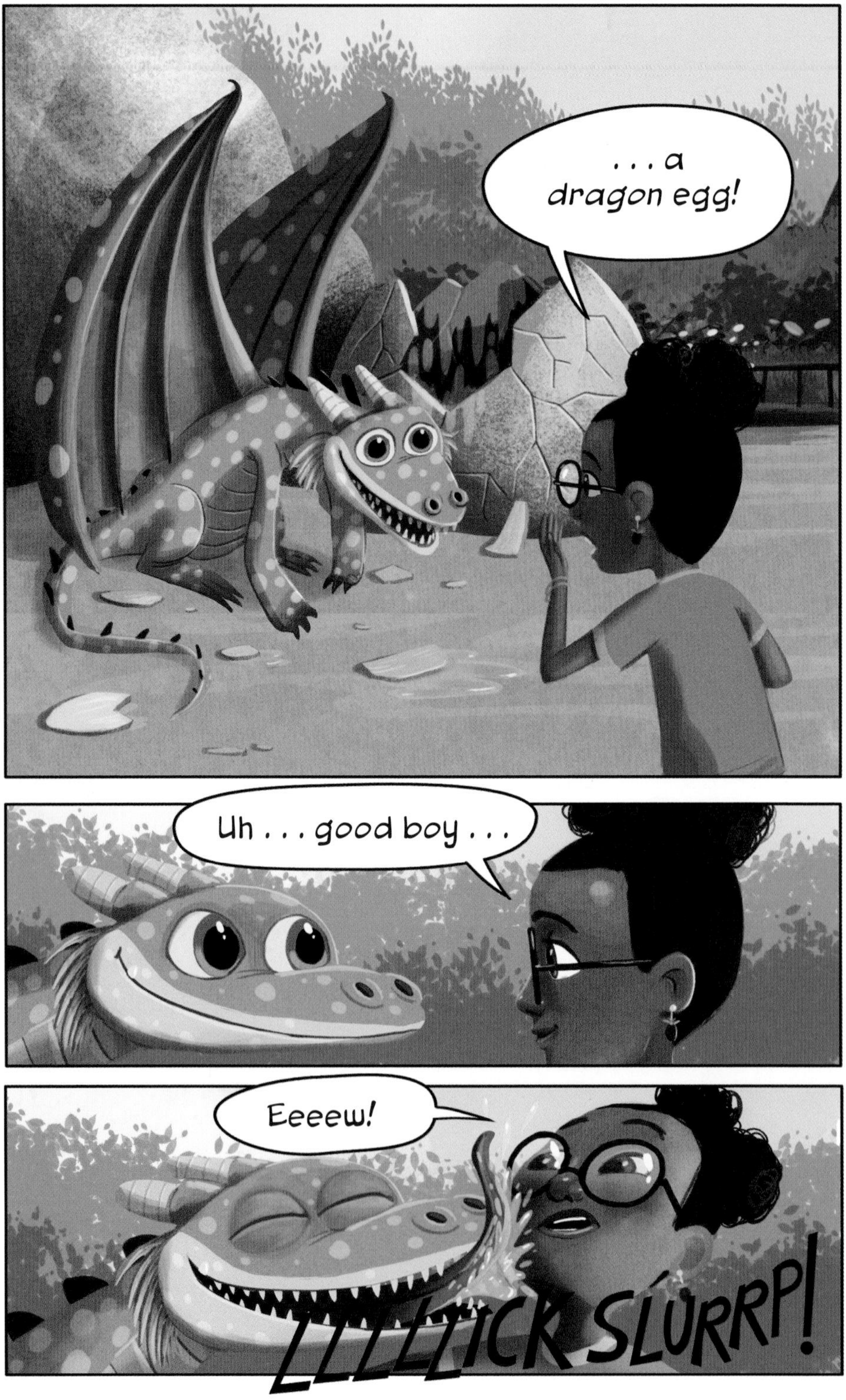
. . . a dragon egg!
Uh . . . good boy . . .
Eeeew!
ZZZZZICK SLURRP!

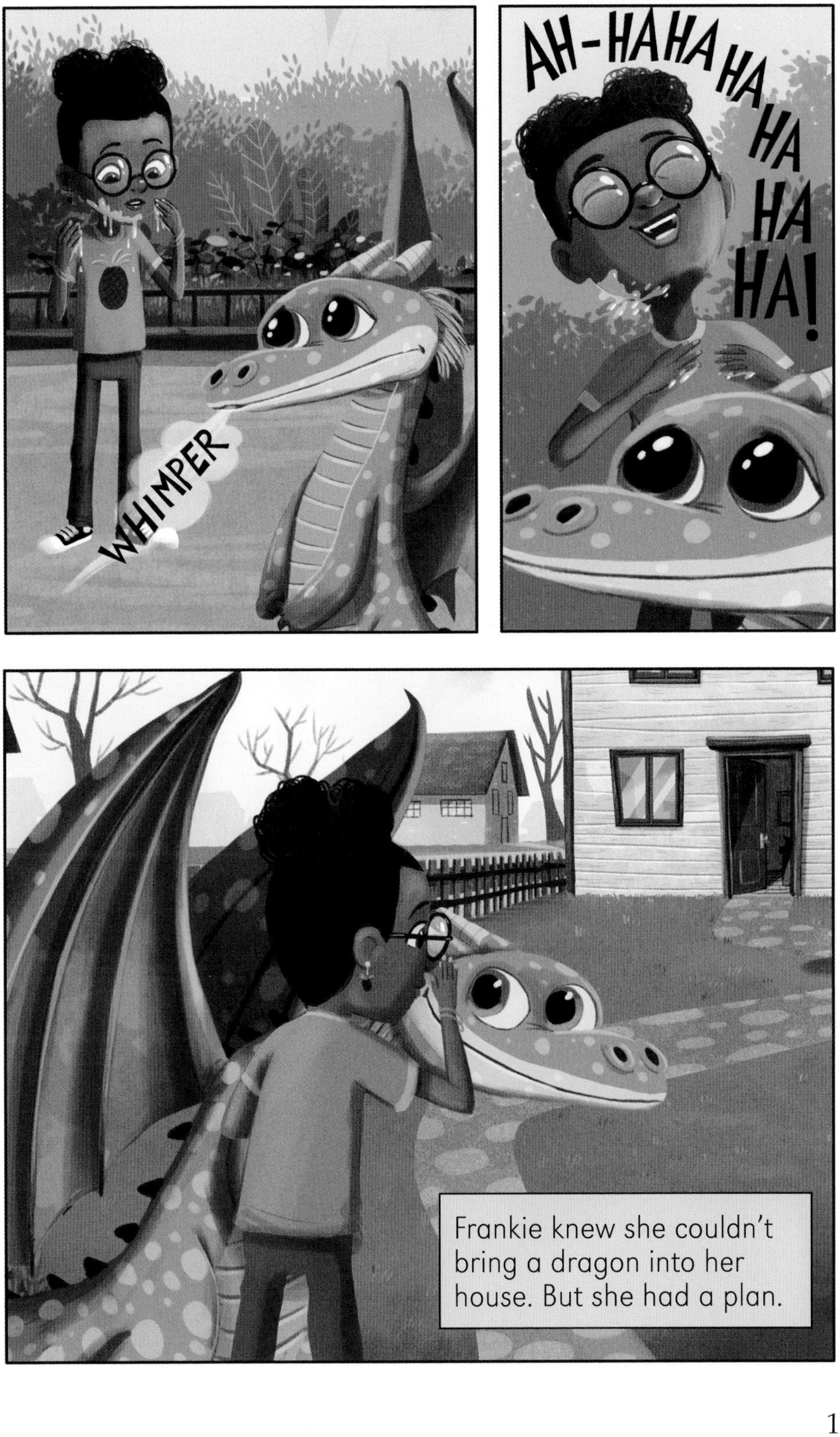
WHIMPER
AH-HAHAHAHAHAHAHA!
Frankie knew she couldn't bring a dragon into her house. But she had a plan.

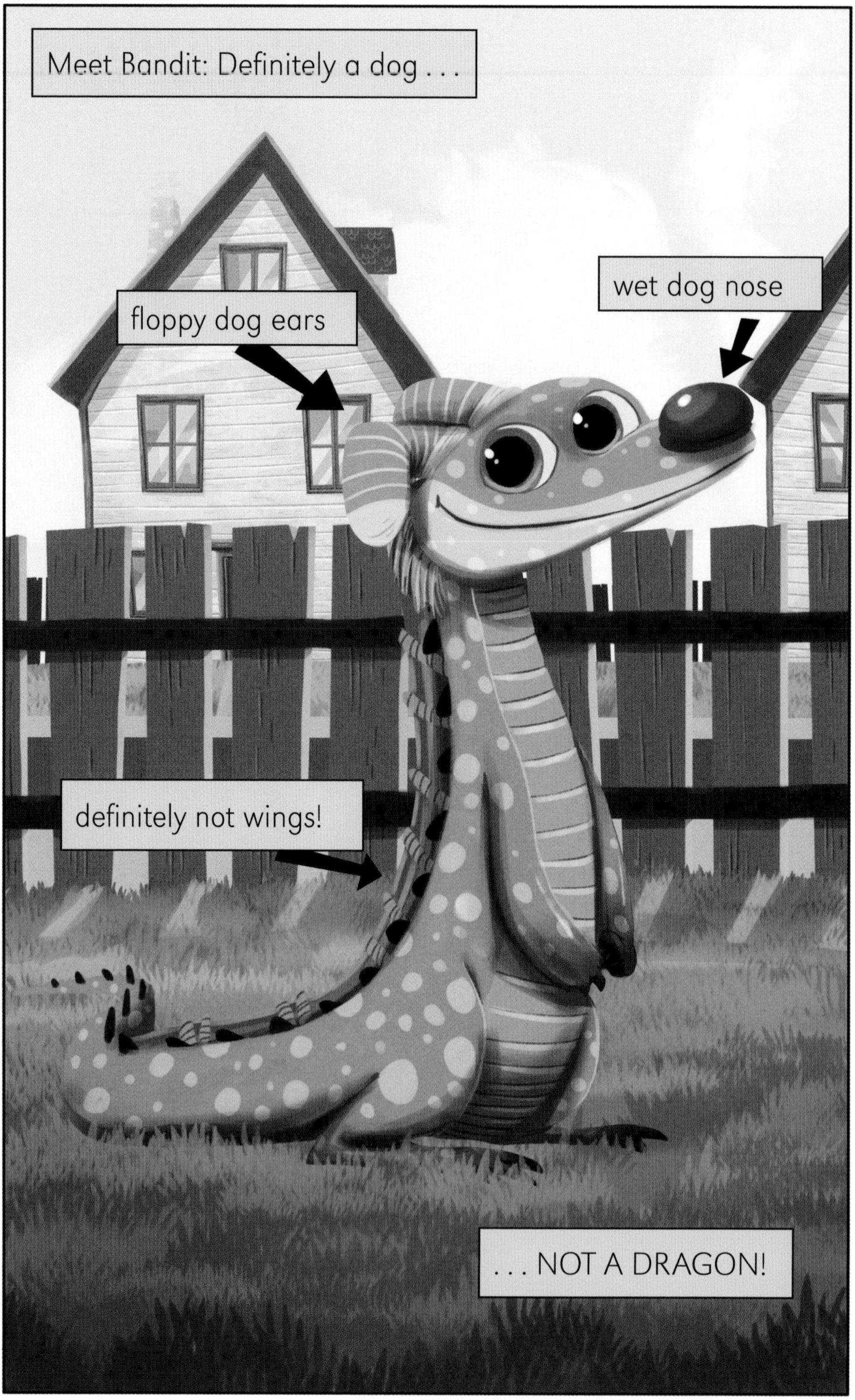
Meet Bandit: Definitely a dog . . .
floppy dog ears
wet dog nose
definitely not wings!
. . . NOT A DRAGON!

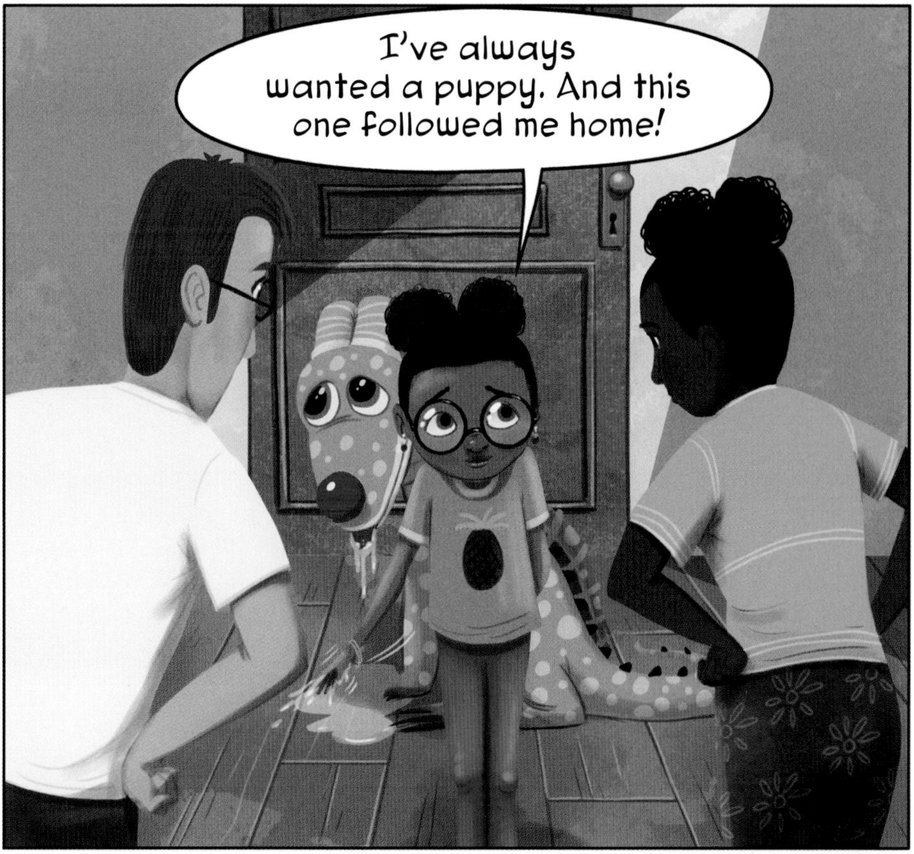
I've always wanted a puppy. And this one followed me home!

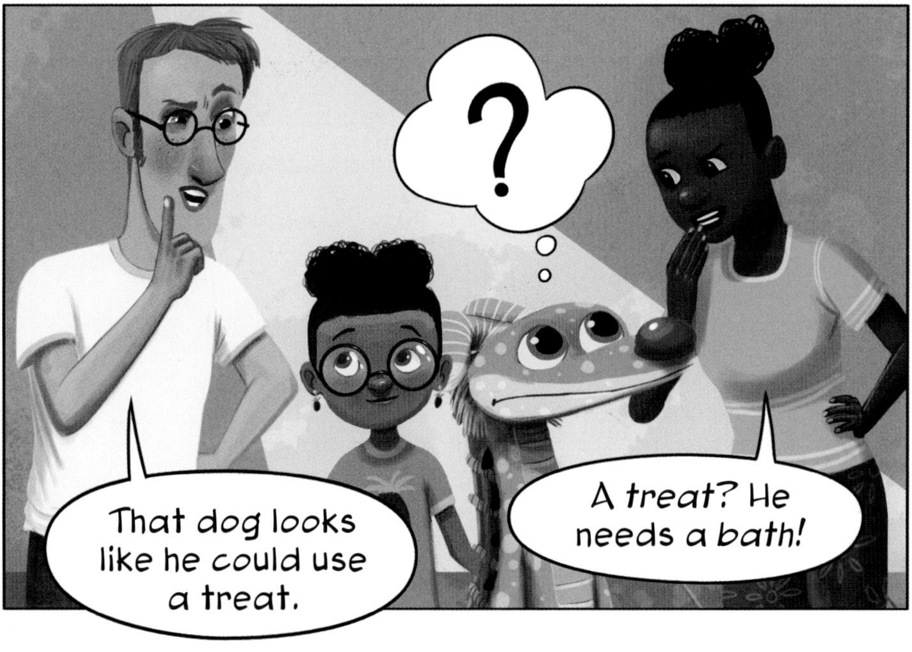
?
That dog looks like he could use a treat.
A *treat*? He needs a *bath*!

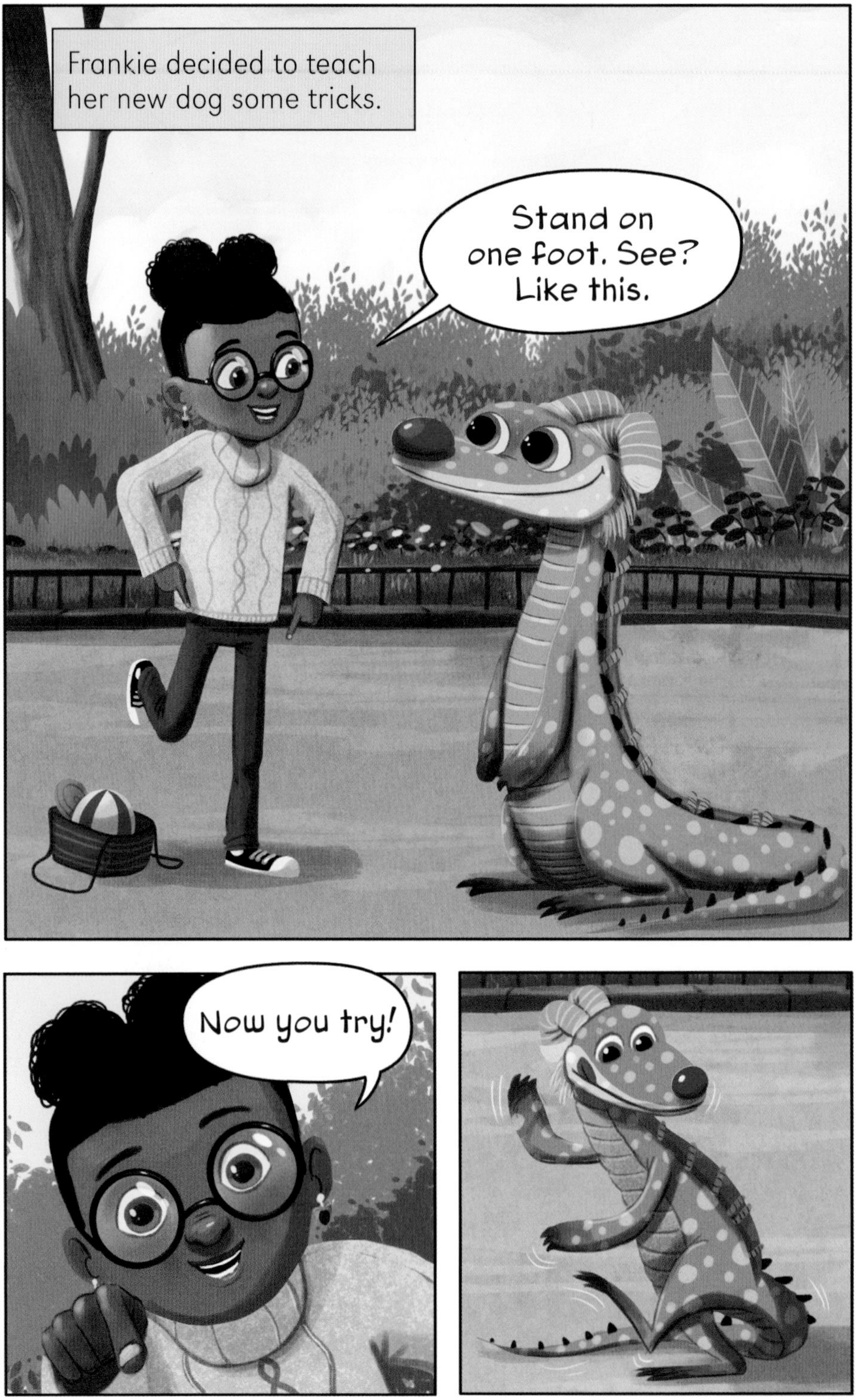
Frankie decided to teach her new dog some tricks.
Stand on one foot. See? Like this.
Now you try!

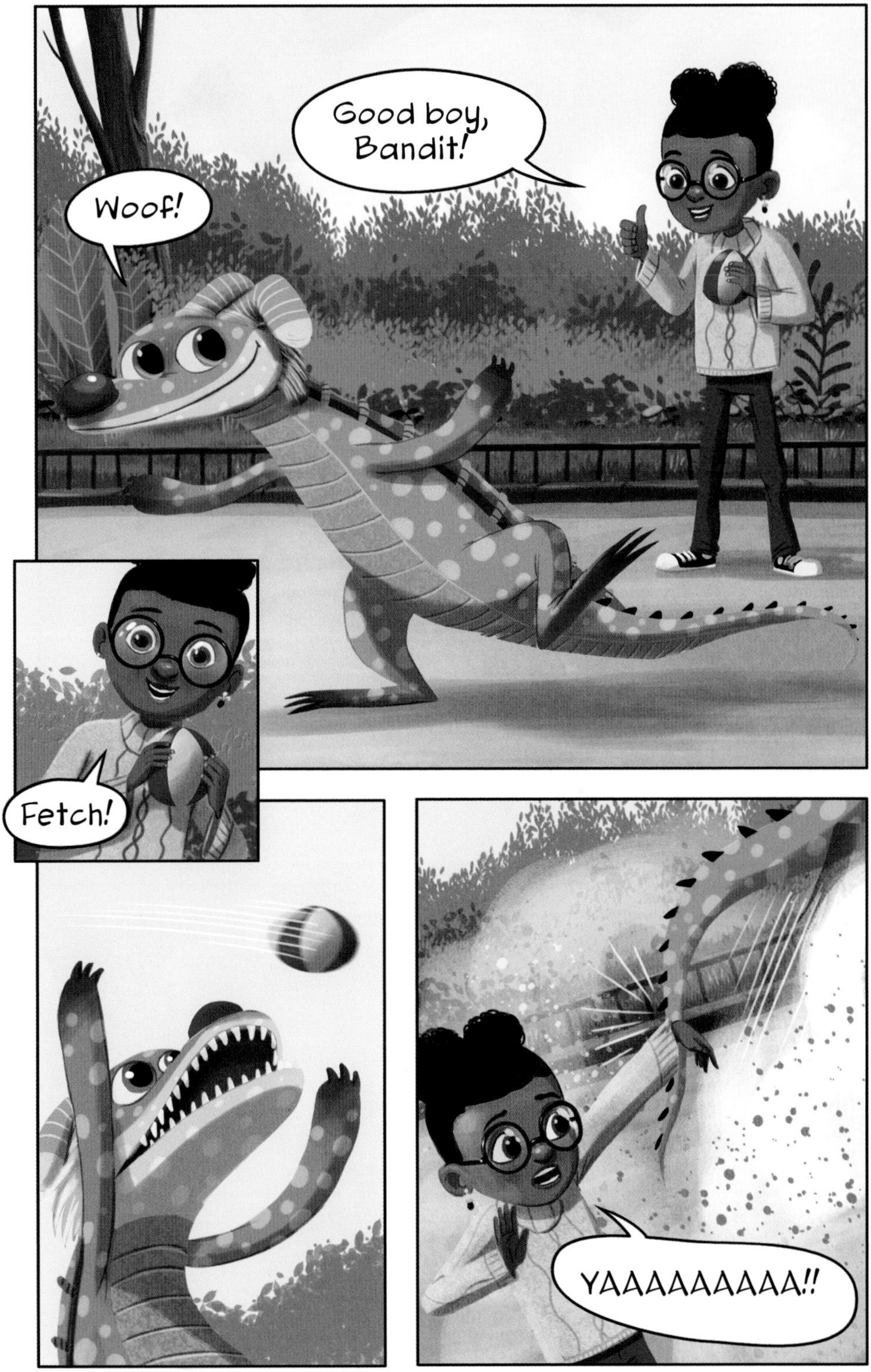
Good boy,
Bandit!
Woof!
Fetch!
YAAAAAAAAA!!

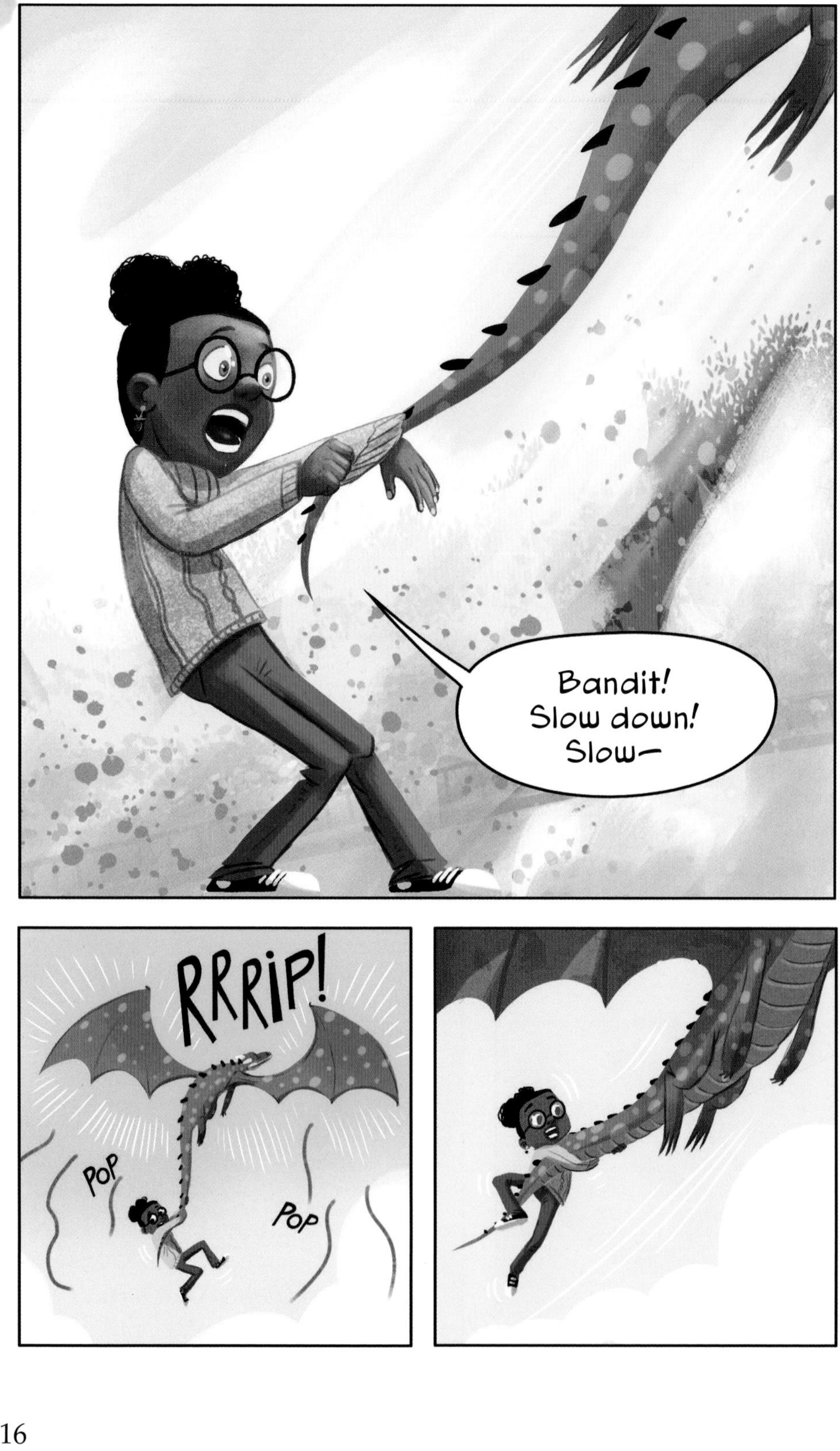
Bandit! Slow down! Slow—
RRRIP!
POP
POP

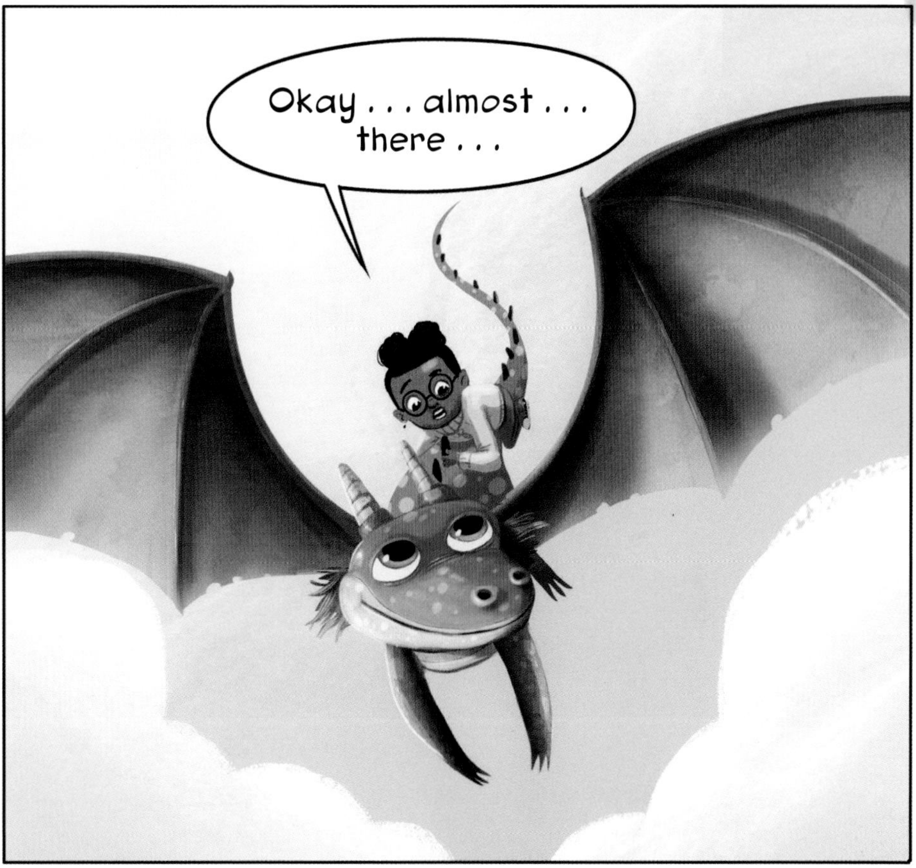
Okay . . . almost . . . there . . .

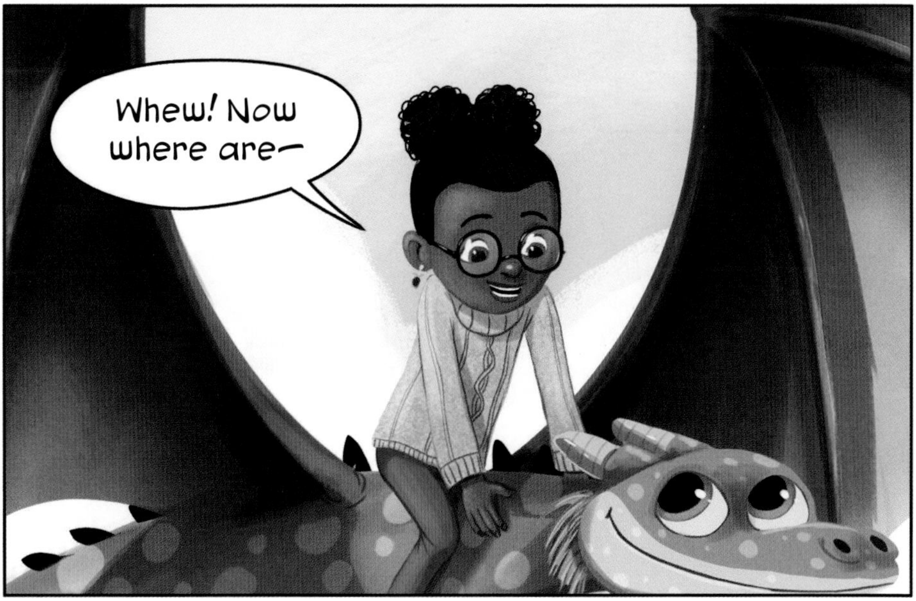
Whew! Now where are—

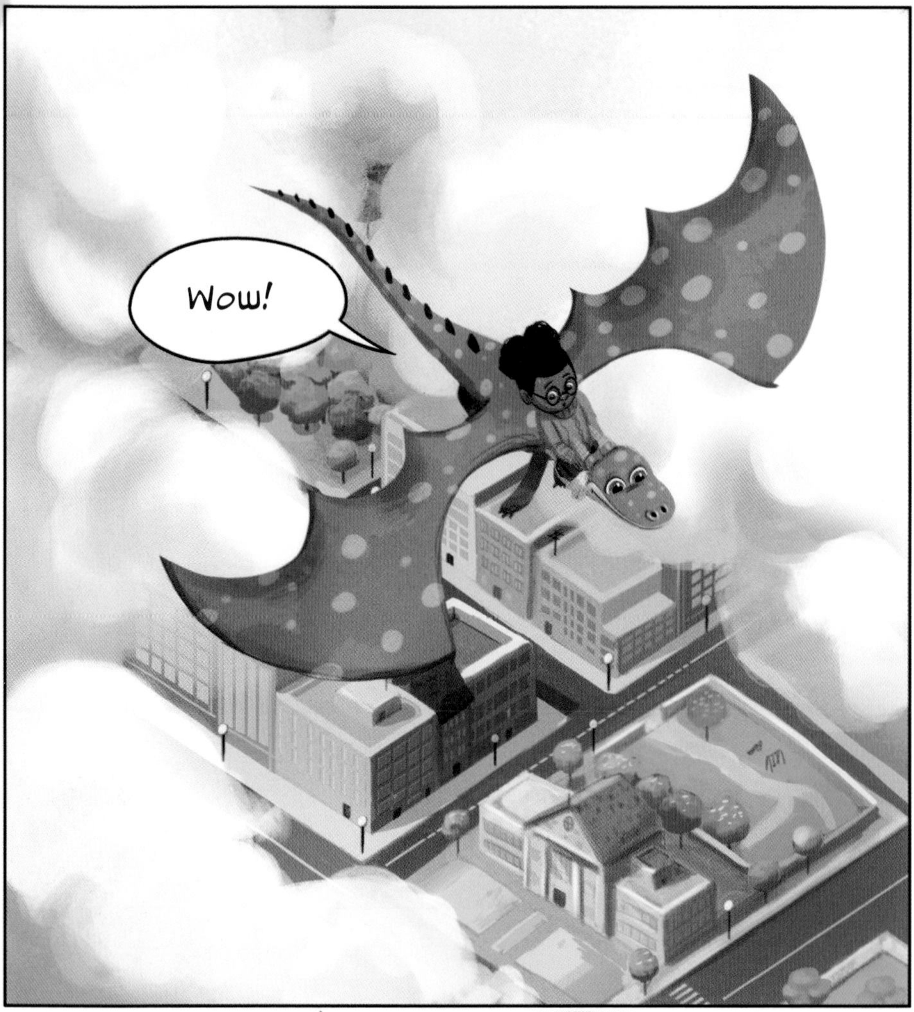
Wow!

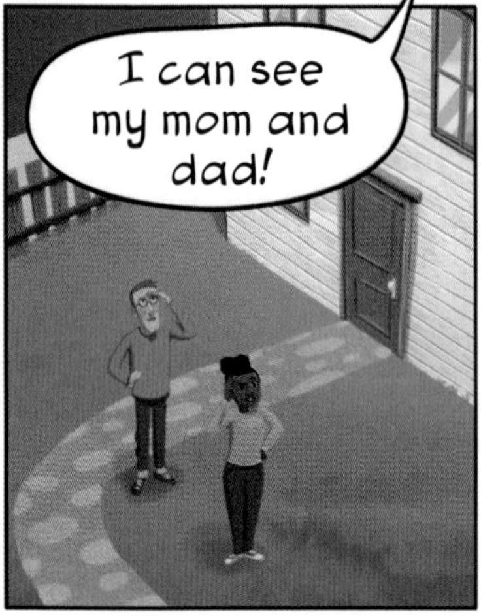
I can see my mom and dad!

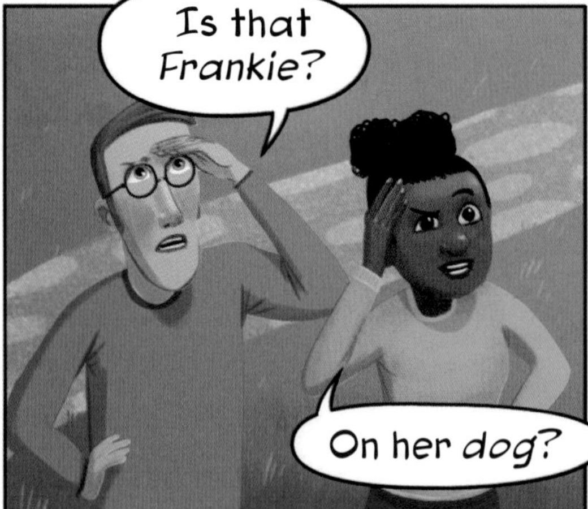
Is that Frankie?
On her dog?

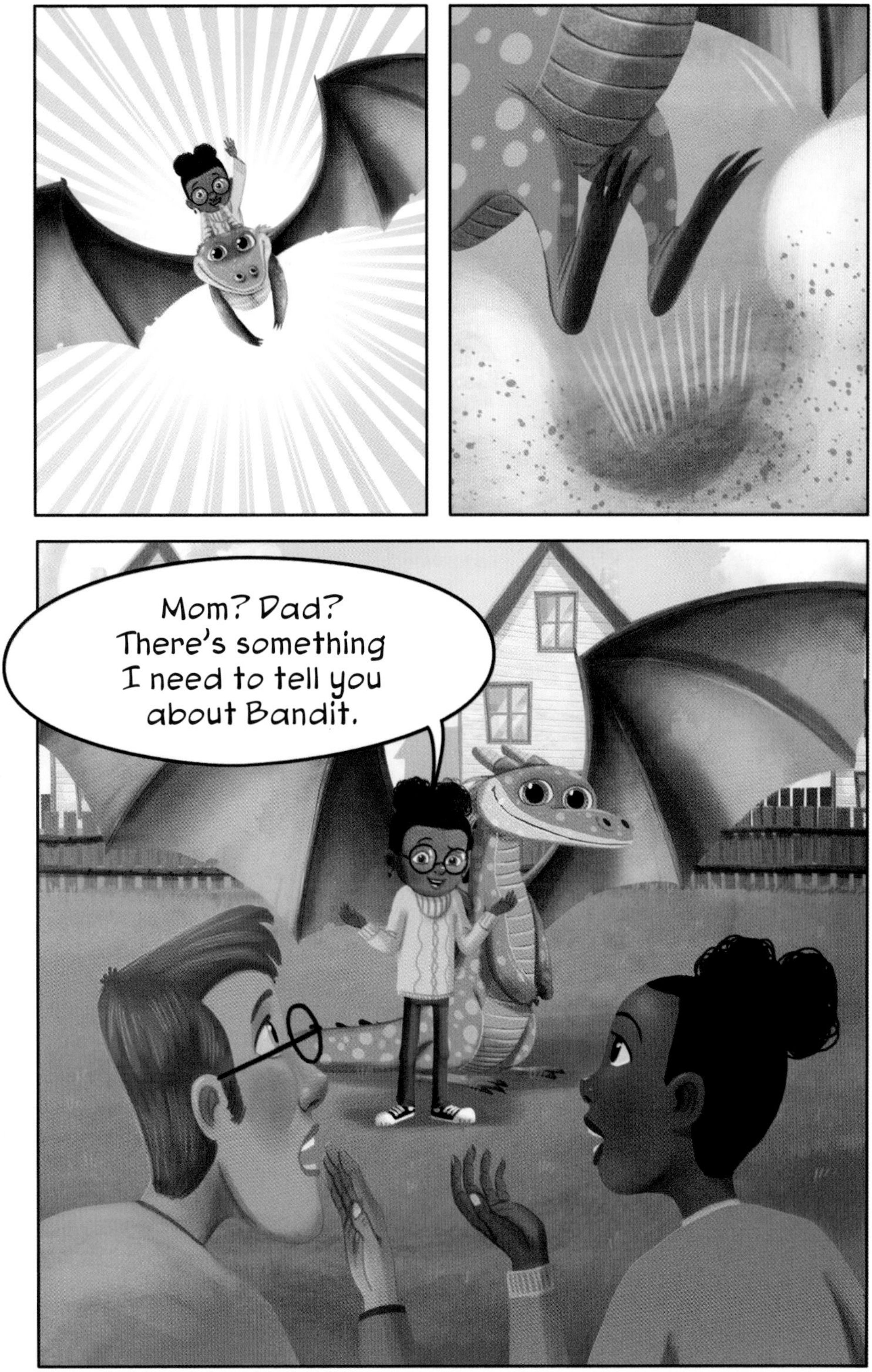
Mom? Dad? There's something I need to tell you about Bandit.

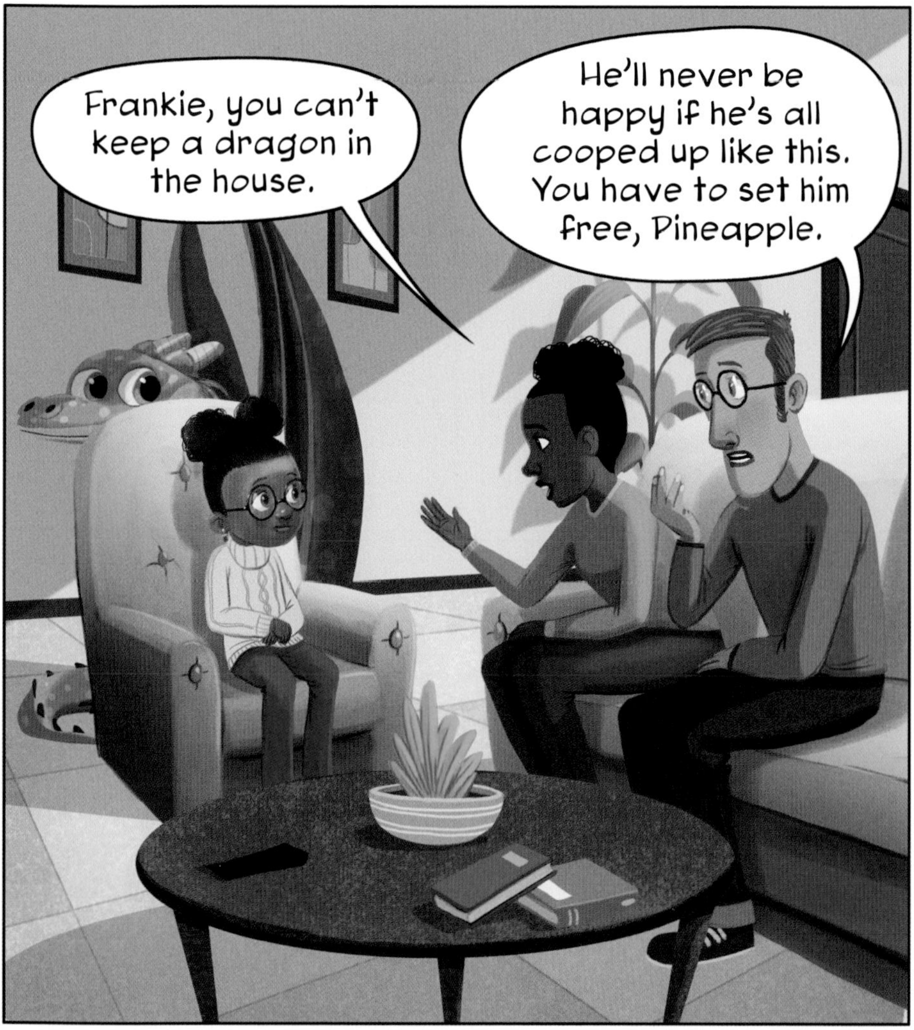
Frankie, you can't keep a dragon in the house.
He'll never be happy if he's all cooped up like this. You have to set him free, Pineapple.

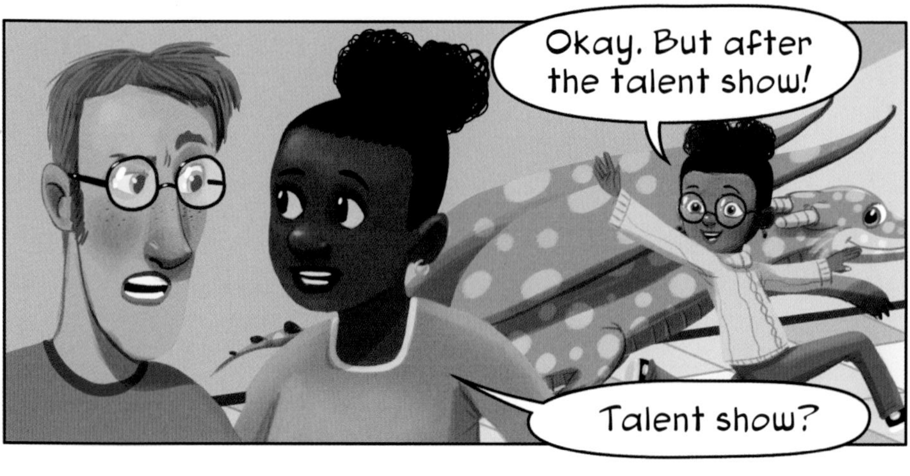
Okay. But after the talent show!
Talent show?

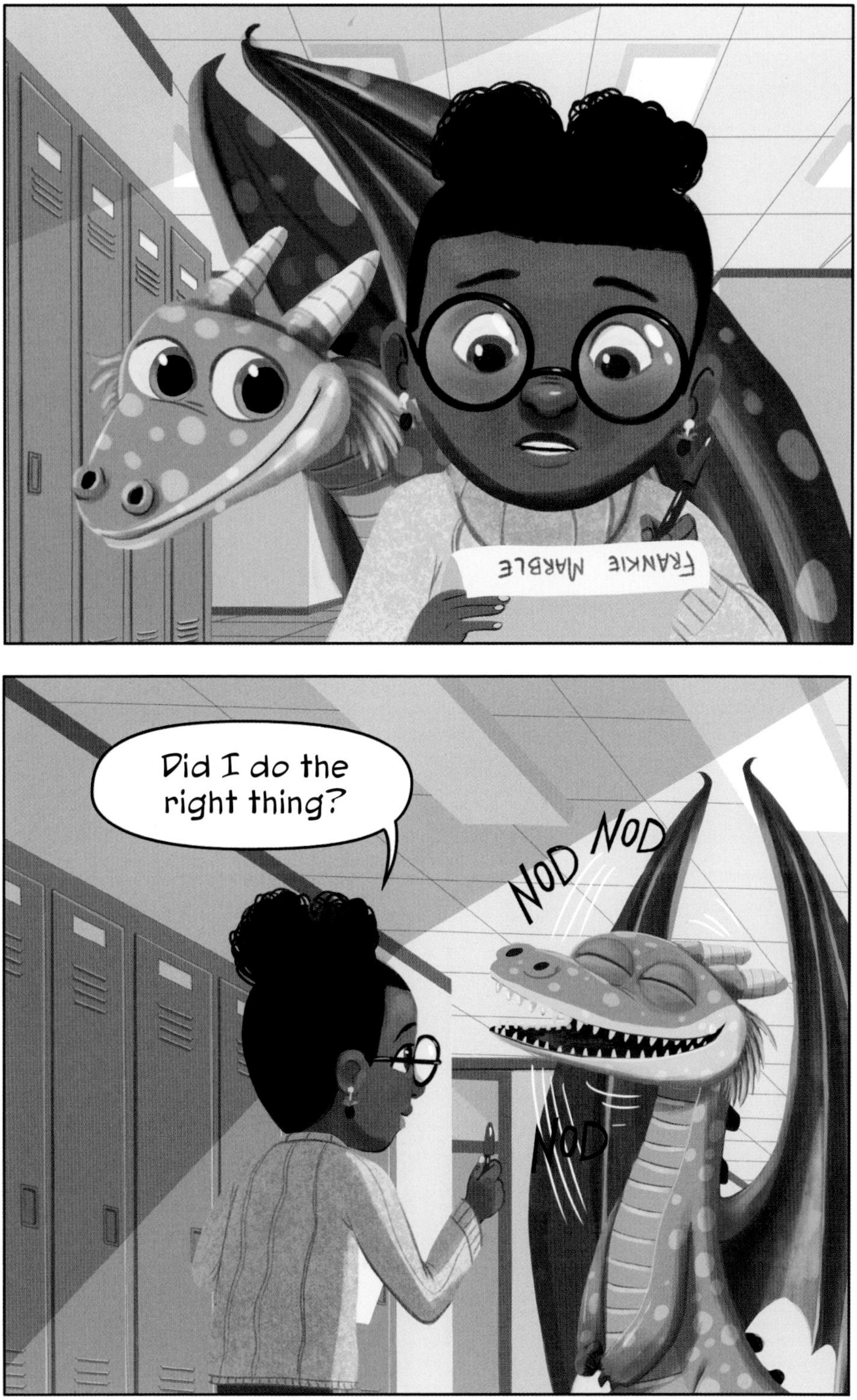
FRANKIE MARBLE
Did I do the right thing?
NOD NOD
NOD

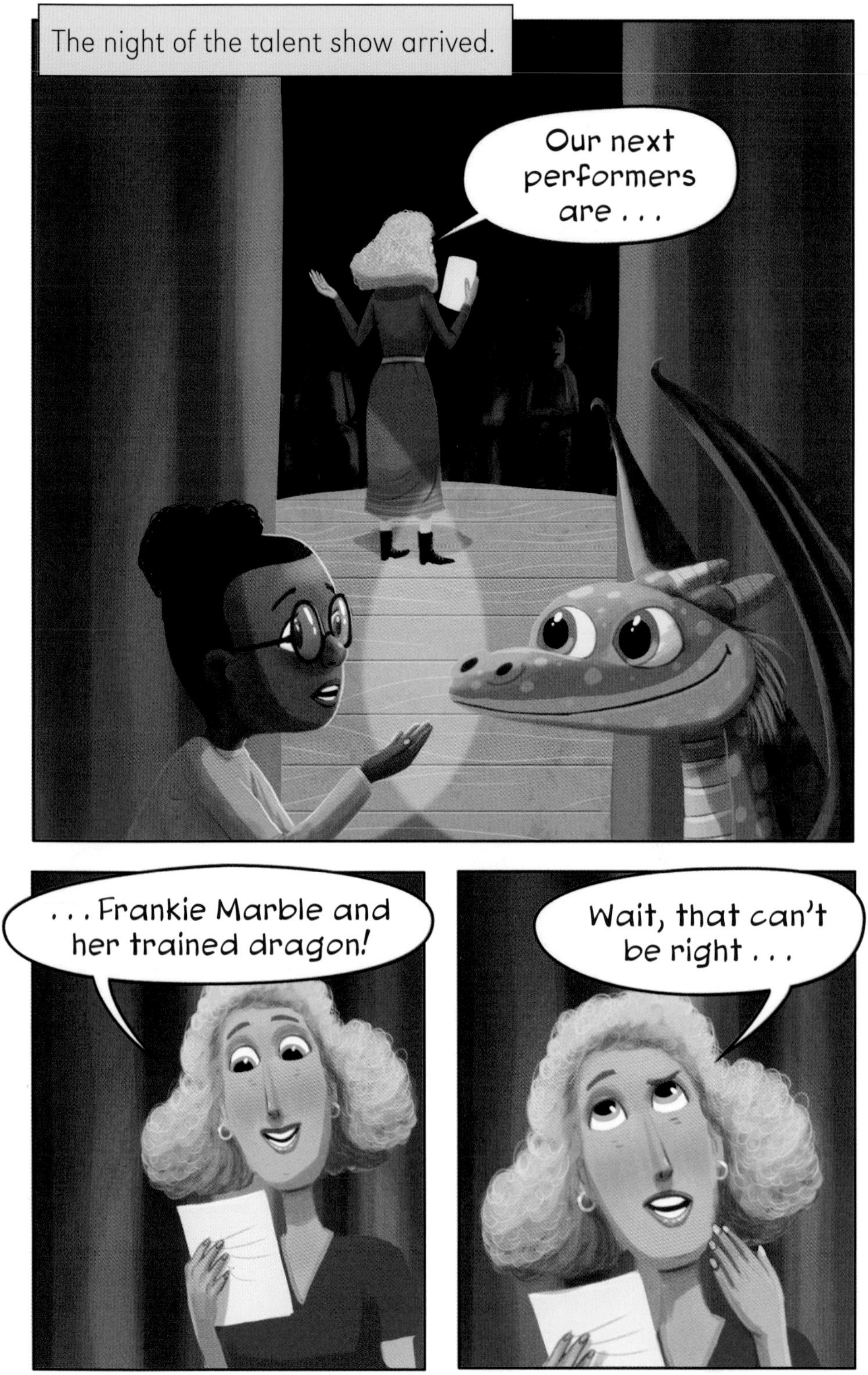
The night of the talent show arrived.
Our next performers are . . .
. . . Frankie Marble and her trained dragon!
Wait, that can't be right . . .

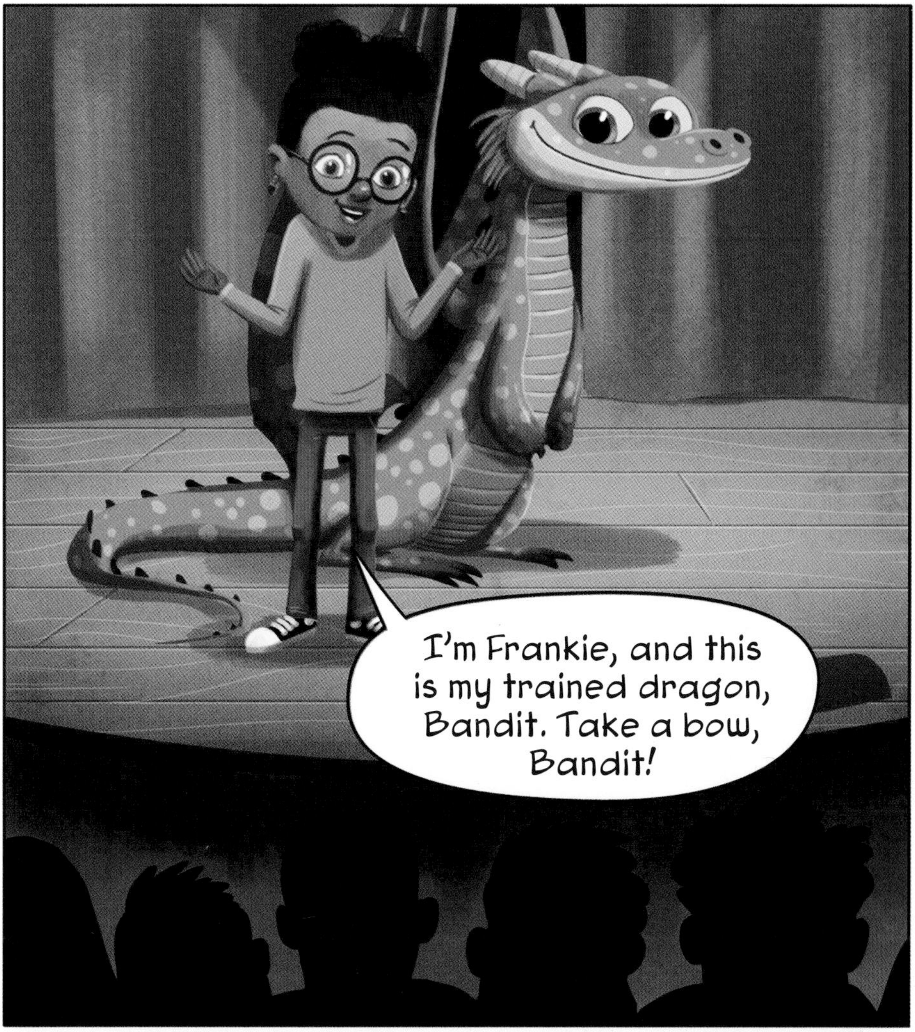
I'm Frankie, and this is my trained dragon, Bandit. Take a bow, Bandit!

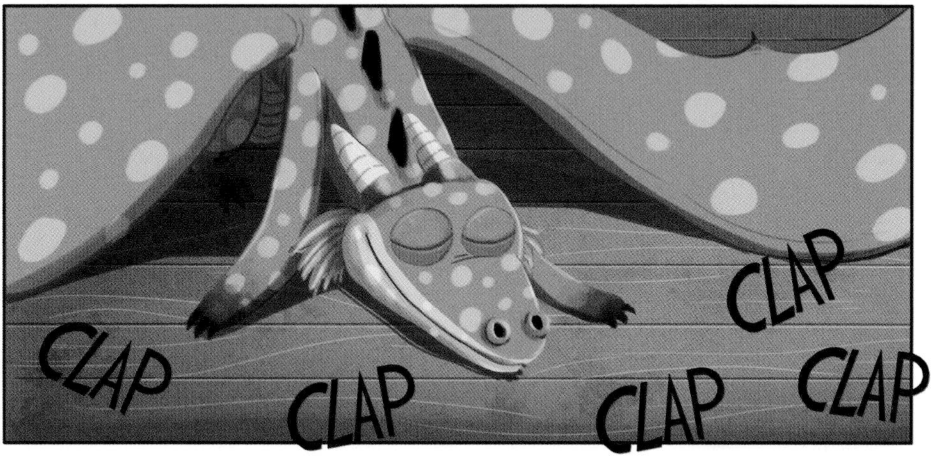
CLAP
CLAP
CLAP
CLAP
CLAP

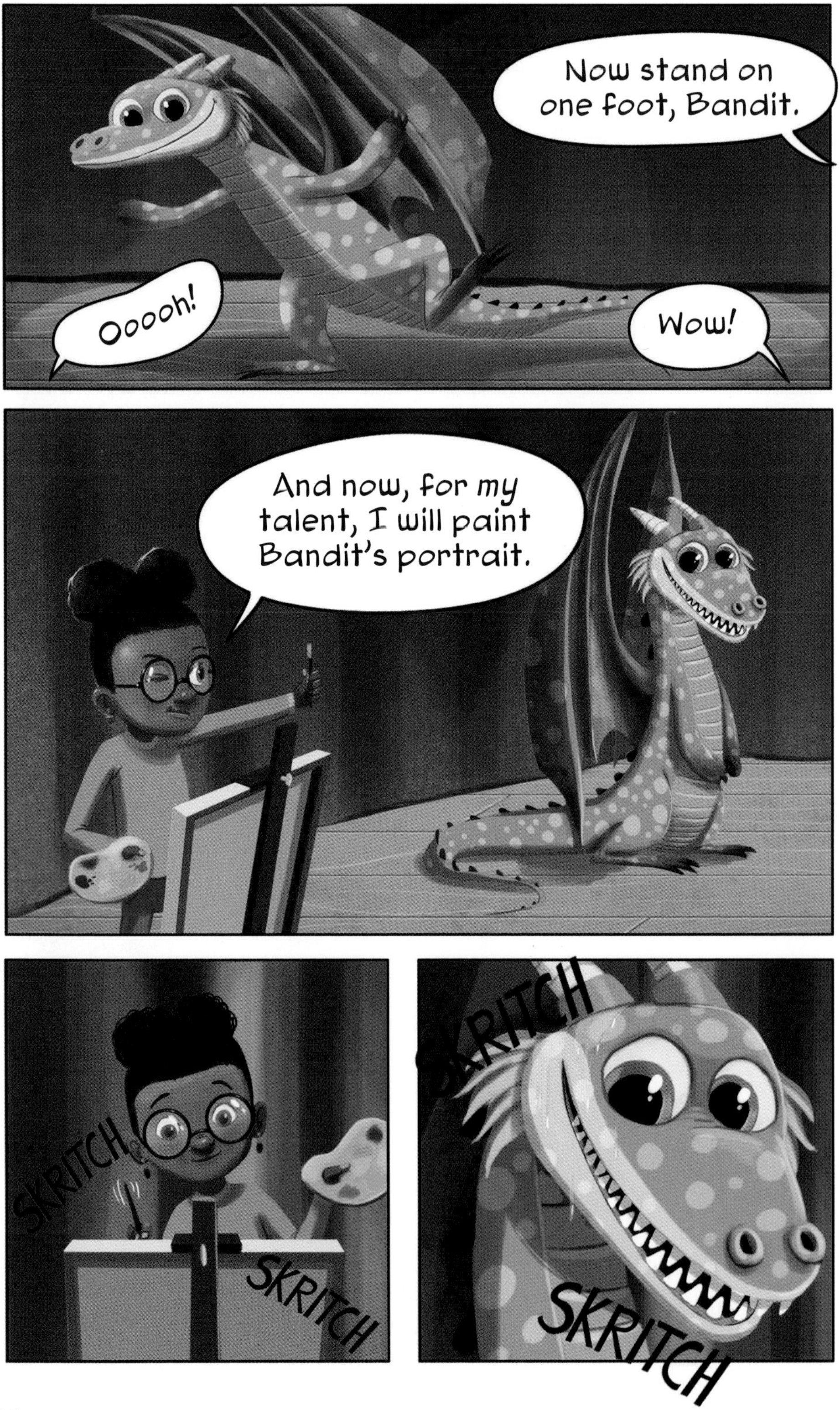
Now stand on one foot, Bandit.
Ooooh!
Wow!
And now, for my talent, I will paint Bandit's portrait.
SKRITCH
SKRITCH
SKRITCH
SKRITCH

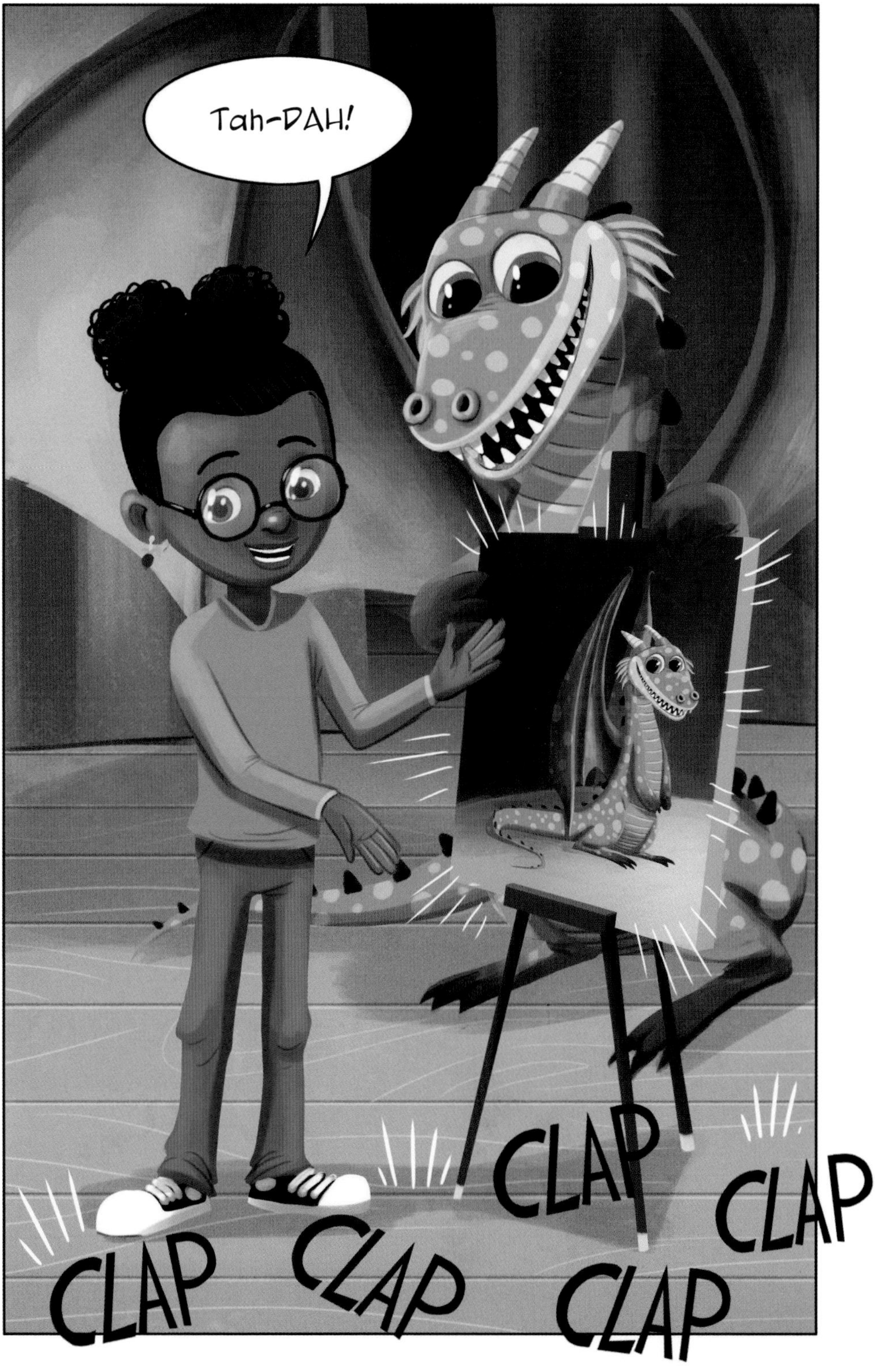
Tah-DAH!
CLAP
CLAP
CLAP
CLAP
CLAP

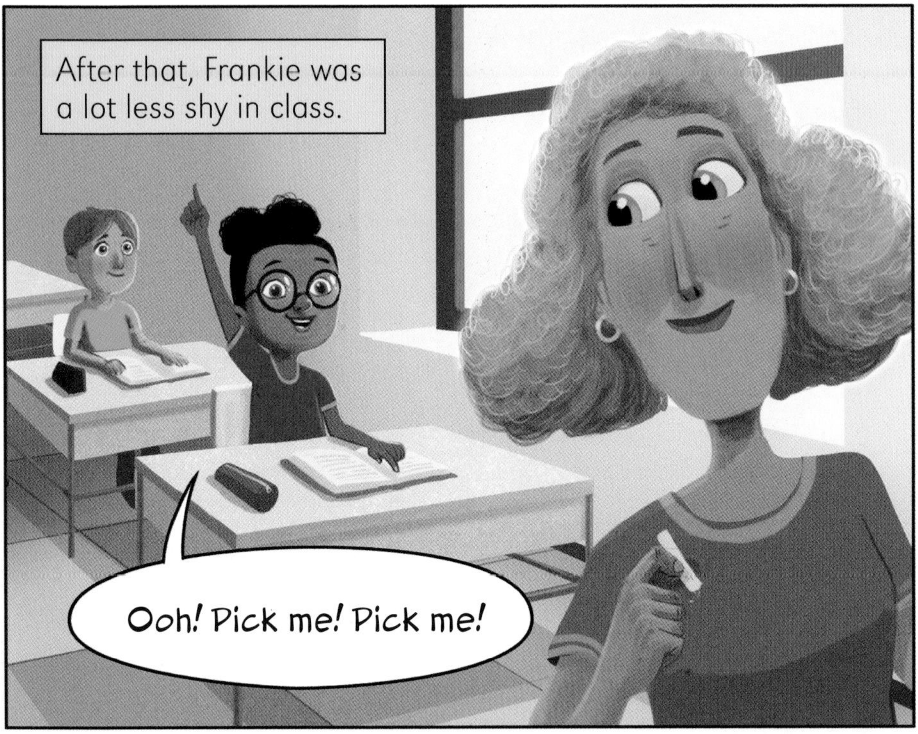
After that, Frankie was a lot less shy in class.
Ooh! Pick me! Pick me!

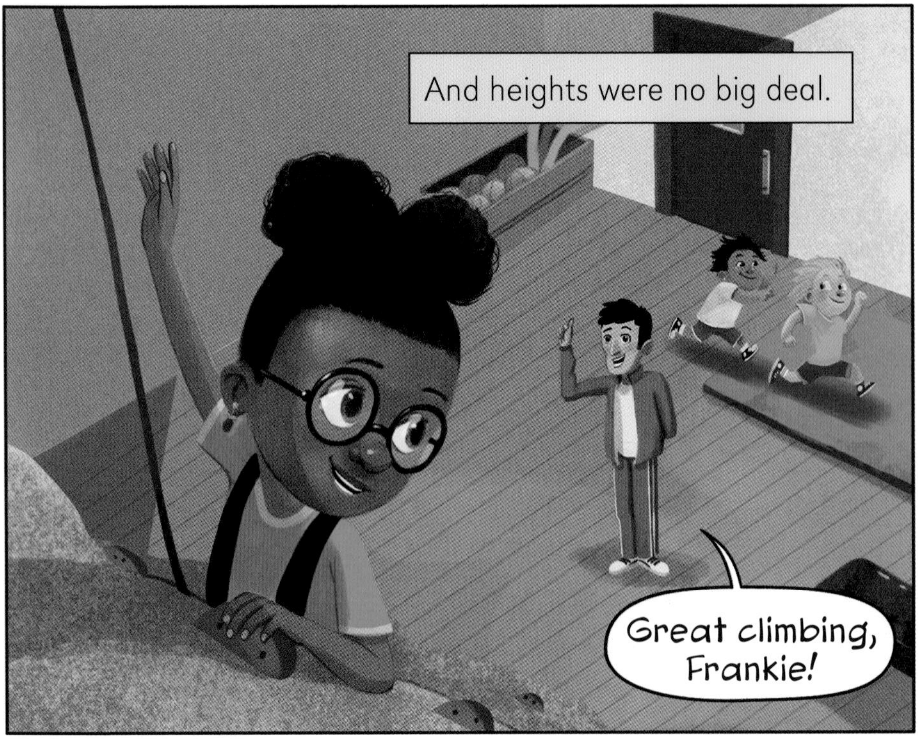
And heights were no big deal.
Great climbing, Frankie!

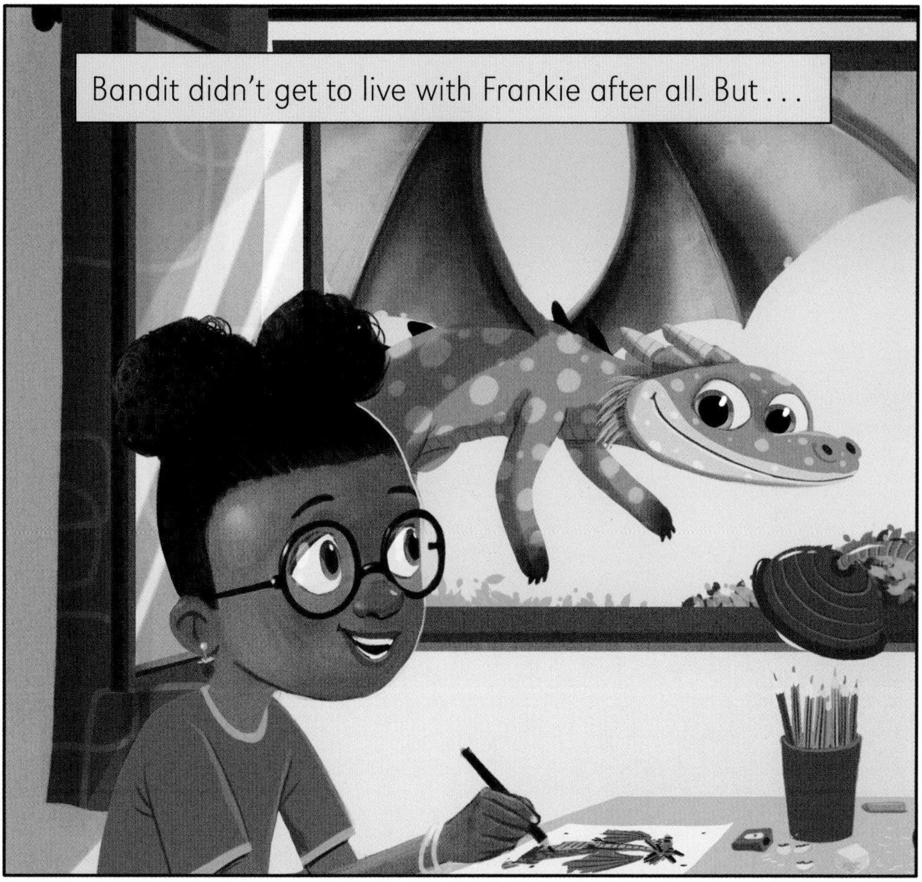
Bandit didn't get to live with Frankie after all. But . . .

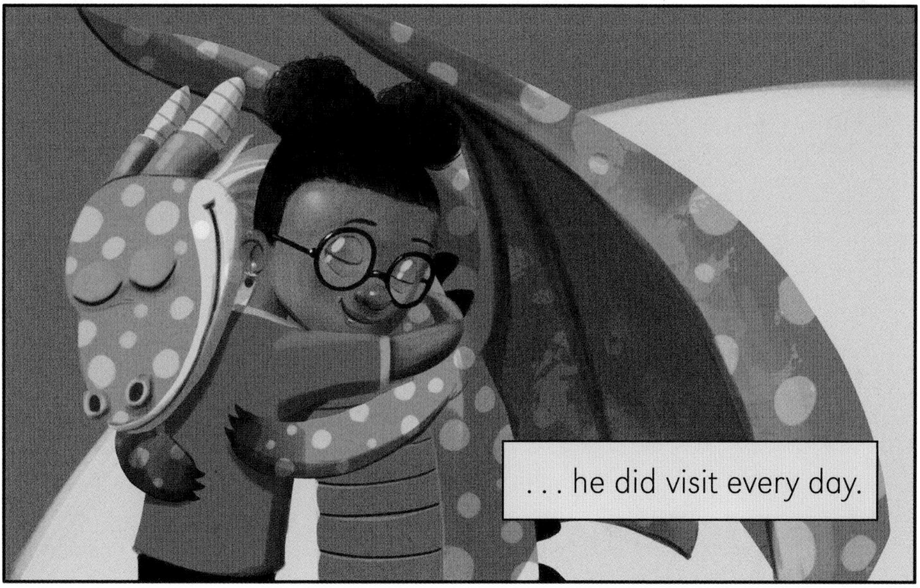
. . . he did visit every day.

WRITING PROMPTS

1. Frankie likes to draw. Do you? Draw a picture of something that happens in the story. Then write a short paragraph to explain what you drew.

2. How do you think Frankie trains Bandit to do tricks? Write a list of instructions on how you would teach a dragon (or a dog) a new trick.

3. Pretend you work for a newspaper. Write a review of the talent show. What would you tell readers you saw at the show?

DISCUSSION QUESTIONS

1. What is Frankie afraid of at the beginning of the story? How does Bandit help her get over those fears?

2. Why doesn't Frankie want to sign up for the school talent show?

3. In what ways has Frankie changed by the end of the story?

MAKE YOUR OWN DRAGON

You can build your own friendly dragon out of everyday objects!

What You Need:
- scissors
- cardboard egg carton
- glue
- square tissue box
- rectangular tissue box
- cardboard paper towel tube
- three sheets of construction paper
- chenille stems
- acrylic paint and paintbrushes

What You Do:

Step 1: With an adult's help, cut two egg cups from the egg carton. Glue them to the top of the square tissue box. This is the dragon's head.

Step 2: Glue the square tissue box to one end of the rectangular tissue box. This is the dragon's body.

Step 3: Ask an adult to cut the paper towel tube into four equal pieces. Glue them to the sides of the rectangular box. These are the dragon's arms and legs.

Step 4: Cut out two hands and two feet from one sheet of construction paper. Glue them onto the open ends of the cardboard tubes.

Step 5: Cut wings out of the second sheet of construction paper.

Step 6: Cut a tail out of the third sheet of construction paper. Then glue the wings and tail onto the dragon.

Step 7: Use the chenille stems to give your dragon features such as horns, antennae, or whiskers.

Step 8: Paint your dragon however you like. What color is your dragon? Does he or she have spots? What color are your dragon's eyes? Does your dragon have huge fangs or itty-bitty teeth?

READ ALL THE AMAZING DISCOVER GRAPHICS BOOKS!

DISCOVER DG GRAPHICS

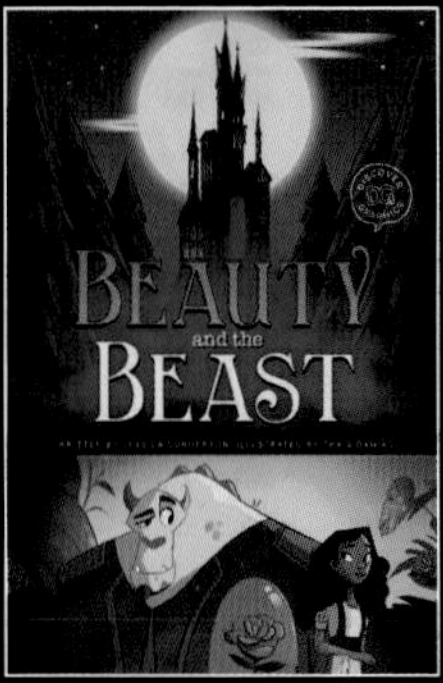
Beauty and the Beast

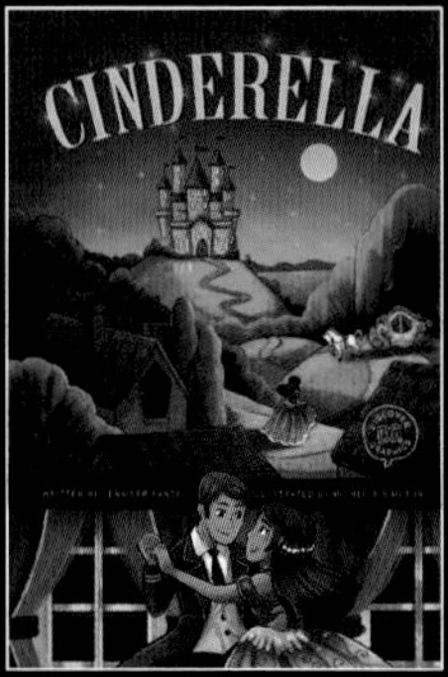
Cinderella

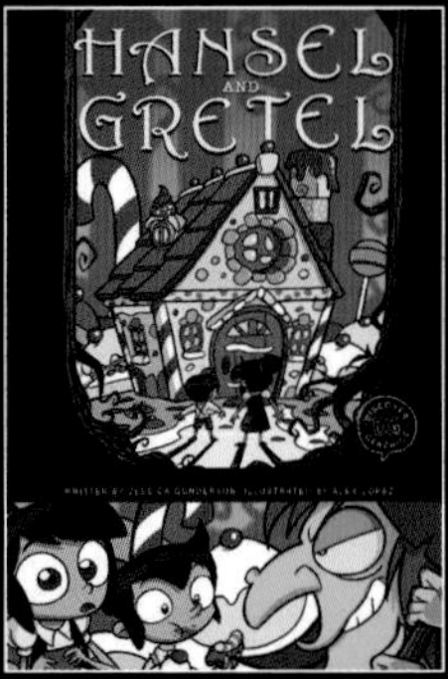
Hansel and Gretel

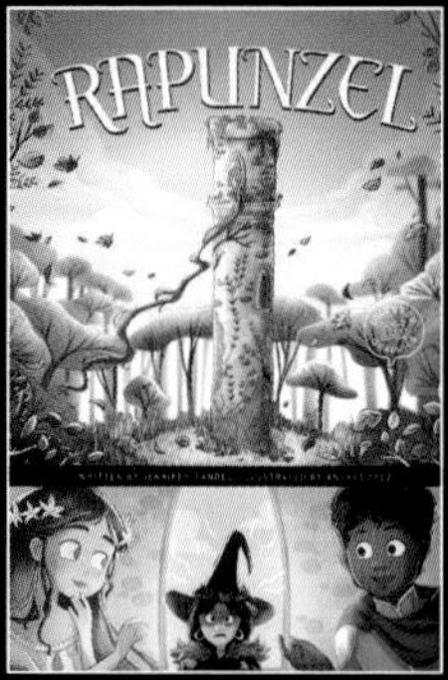
Rapunzel

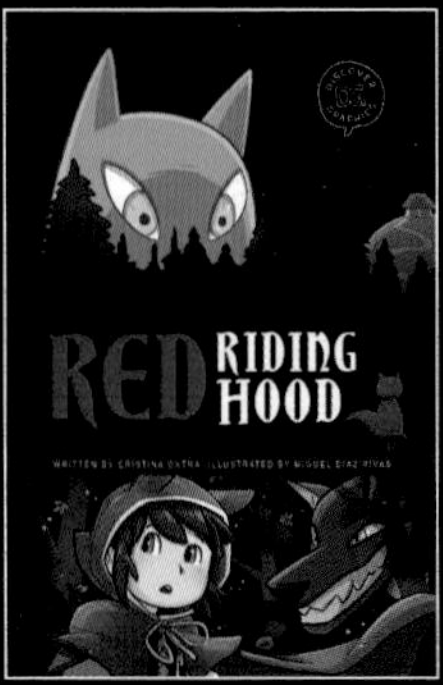
Red Riding Hood

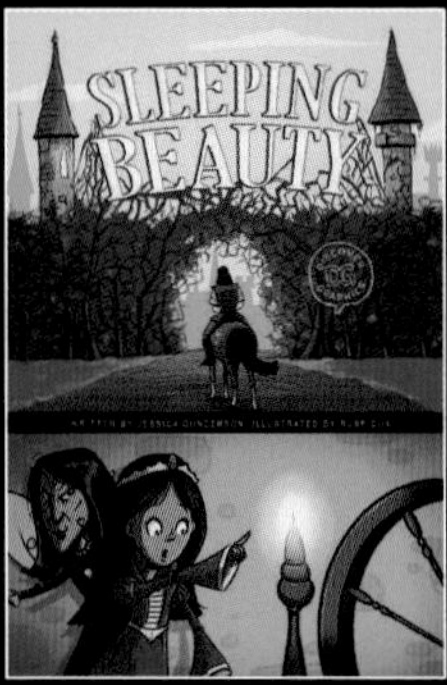
Sleeping Beauty

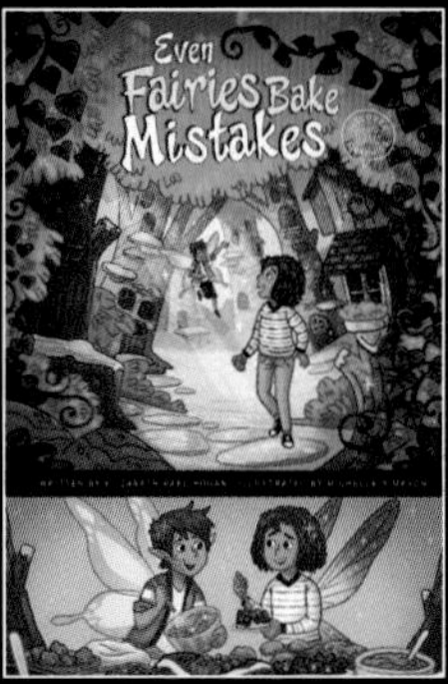
Even Fairies Bake Mistakes

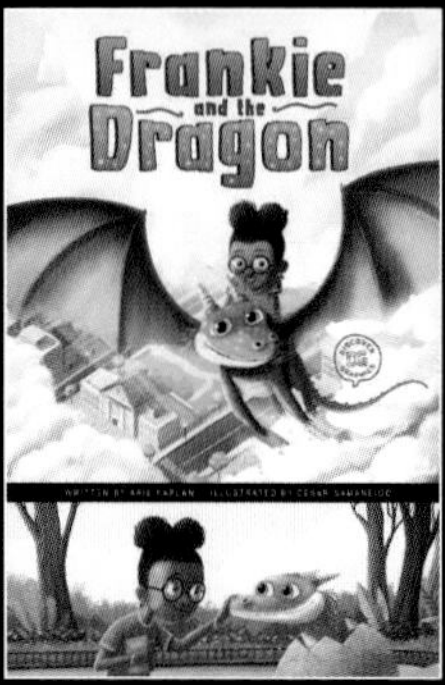
Frankie and the Dragon

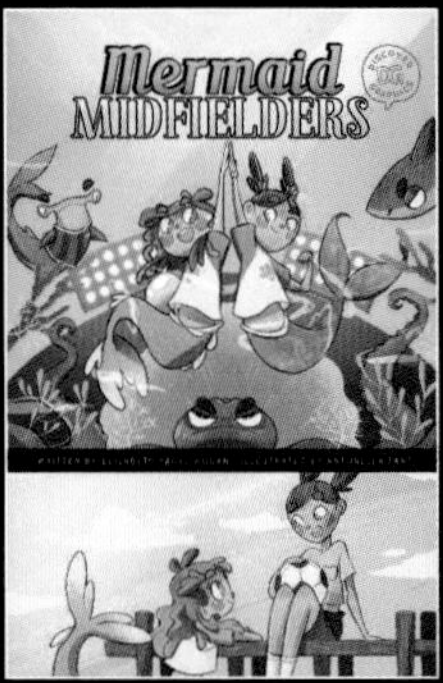
Mermaid Midfielders

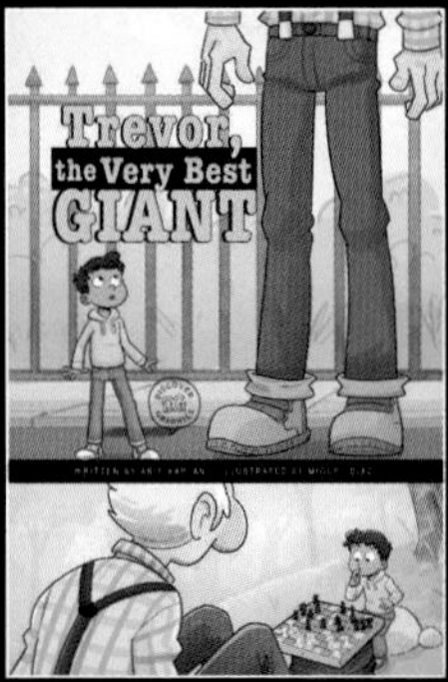
Trevor, the Very Best Giant

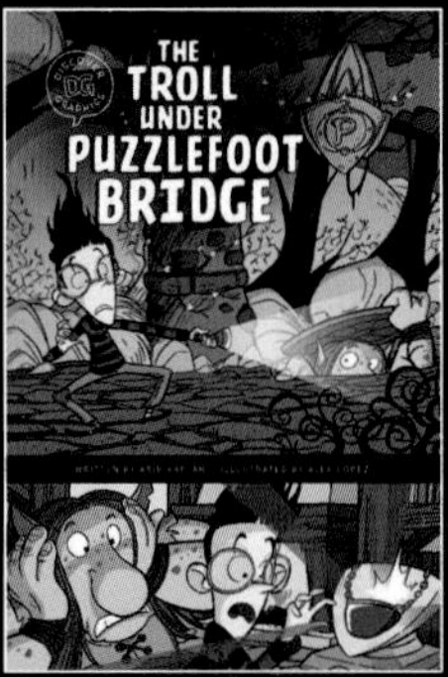
The Troll Under Puzzlefoot Bridge

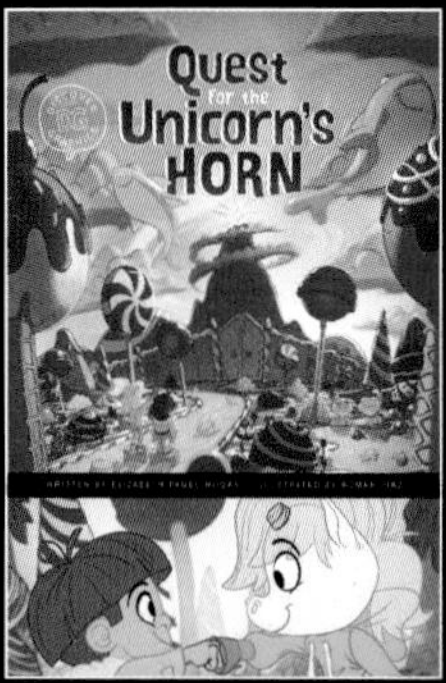
Quest for the Unicorn's Horn